withdrawn

WELCOME, KIND READER, TO A TALE OF ASGARD...

Thor, the prince of Asgard, is a brash and impetuous youth. Never one to consider who he is or what he has, Thor's mind is always on who he will one day be and what the future holds for him. He feels he lives in the shadow of his father, Odin, ruler of all Asgard, and he hopes he can escape that fate through noble deeds and valiant acts.

When Odin asks Thor and his fellow young warriors, Balder and Sif, to undertake a quest on his behalf, Thor quickly agrees, but does not consult his friends. Though Sif and Balder are angered by Thor's inconsiderate behavior, they commit themselves to the task at hand. Together the trio travels Asgard in search of four mystic elements which Odin hopes to forge into an enchanted sword.

They have defeated the dragon Hakurei and removed one of the scales from his armored hide. They have battled ice pixies on the frozen peaks of Jotunheim in order to obtain a feather from the snow eagle Gnori. And they have overcome the vicious Jennia deep beneath the sands of the Asgardian desert to win a magic jewel. Now, only the fourth element remains- enchanted water from the mystic Lake of Lilitha...

PART FIVE
THE LAKE OF LILITHA

AKIRA YOSHIDA
WRITER

GREG TOCCHINI
PENCILER

JAY LEISTEN
INKER

GURU eFX
COLORIST

VC's RANDY GENTILE
LETTERER

ADI GRANOV
COVER ARTIST

MACKENZIE CADENHEAD
EDITOR

RALPH MACCHIO & C.B. CEBULSKI
CONSULTING EDITORS

JOE QUESADA
EDITOR IN CHIEF

DAN BUCKLEY
PUBLISHER

MARVEL®   Spotlight

VISIT US AT
www.abdopublishing.com

Reinforced library bound edition published in 2007 by Spotlight, a division of the ABDO Publishing Group, Edina, Minnesota. Spotlight produces high quality reinforced library bound editions for schools and libraries. Published by agreement with Marvel Characters, Inc.

Library of Congress Cataloging-in-Publication Data

Yoshida, Akira.
Thor, son of Asgard / [Akira Yoshida, writer ; Greg Tocchini, penciler ; Jay Leisten, inker ; Guru e FX, colorist ; Adi Granov, cover artist ; Randy Gentile, letterer].
p. cm.
Cover title.
"Marvel Age."
Revisions of issues 1-6 of the serial Thor, son of Asgard.
Contents: pt. 1. The warriors teen -- pt. 2. The heat of Hakurei -- pt. 3. The nest of Gnori -- pt. 4. The jaws of Jennia -- pt. 5. The lake of Lilitha -- pt. 6. The trio triumphant.
ISBN-13: 978-1-59961-286-7 (pt. 1)
ISBN-10: 1-59961-286-0 (pt. 1)
ISBN-13: 978-1-59961-287-4 (pt. 2)
ISBN-10: 1-59961-287-9 (pt. 2)
ISBN-13: 978-1-59961-288-1 (pt. 3)
ISBN-10: 1-59961-288-7 (pt. 3)
ISBN-13: 978-1-59961-289-8 (pt. 4)
ISBN-10: 1-59961-289-5 (pt. 4)
ISBN-13: 978-1-59961-290-4 (pt. 5)
ISBN-10: 1-59961-290-9 (pt. 5)
ISBN-13: 978-1-59961-291-1 (pt. 6)
ISBN-10: 1-59961-291-7 (pt. 6)
1. Comic books, strips, etc. I. Tocchini, Greg. II. Title. III. Title: Warriors teen. IV. Title: Heat of Hakurei. V. Title: Nest of Gnori. VI. Title: Jaws of Jennia. VII. Title: Lake of Lilitha. VIII. Title: Trio triumphant.

PN6728.T64Y68 2007
791.5'73--dc22

2006050635

Spotlight

All Spotlight books are reinforced library binding
and manufactured in the United States of America.

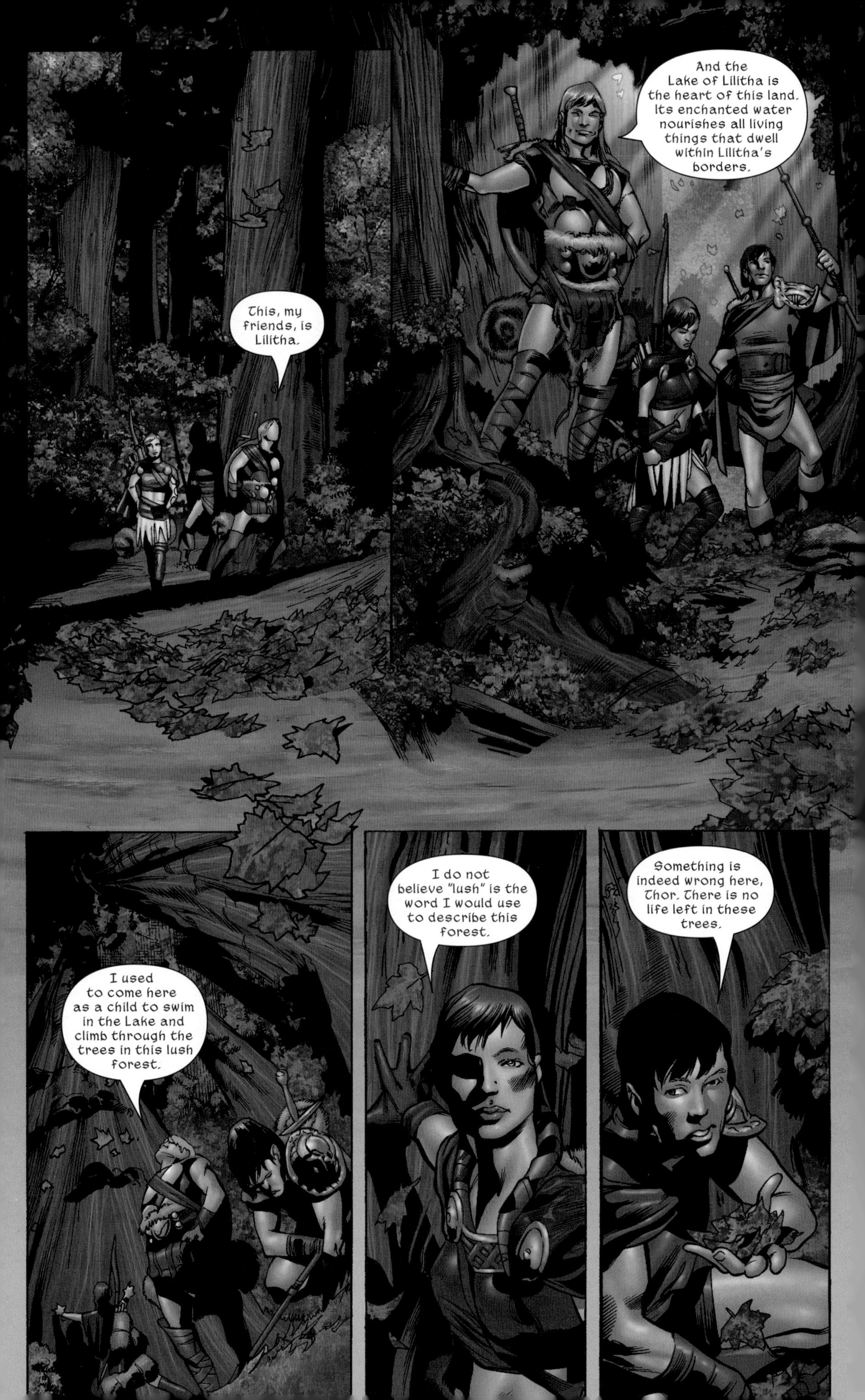
This, my friends, is Lilitha.
And the Lake of Lilitha is the heart of this land. Its enchanted water nourishes all living things that dwell within Lilitha's borders.
I used to come here as a child to swim in the Lake and climb through the trees in this lush forest.
I do not believe "lush" is the word I would use to describe this forest.
Something is indeed wrong here, Thor. There is no life left in these trees.

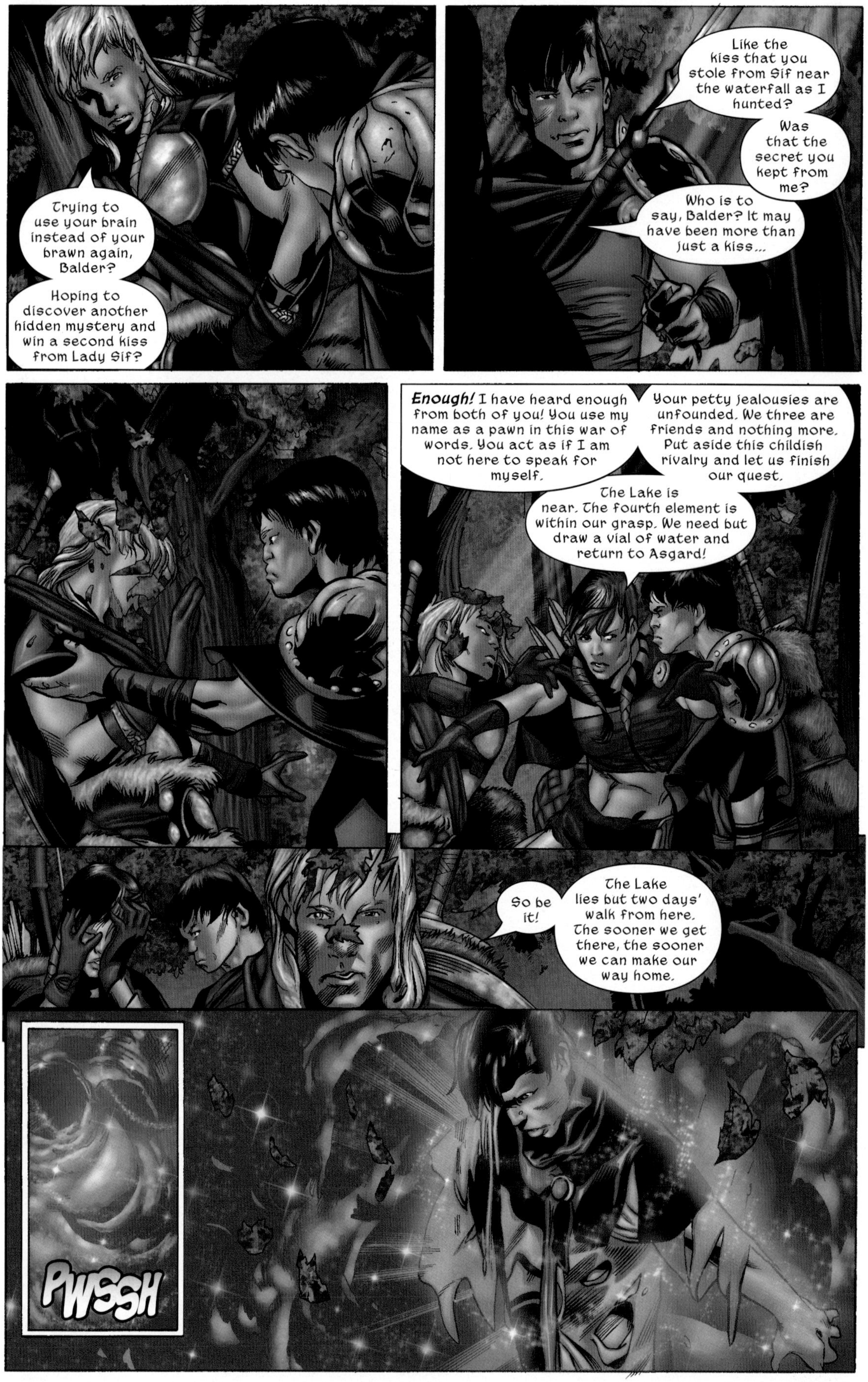
Trying to use your brain instead of your brawn again, Balder?
Hoping to discover another hidden mystery and win a second kiss from Lady Sif?
Like the kiss that you stole from Sif near the waterfall as I hunted?
Was that the secret you kept from me?
Who is to say, Balder? It may have been more than just a kiss...
Enough! I have heard enough from both of you! You use my name as a pawn in this war of words. You act as if I am not here to speak for myself.
Your petty jealousies are unfounded. We three are friends and nothing more. Put aside this childish rivalry and let us finish our quest.
The Lake is near. The fourth element is within our grasp. We need but draw a vial of water and return to Asgard!
So be it!
The Lake lies but two days' walk from here. The sooner we get there, the sooner we can make our way home.
PWSSH

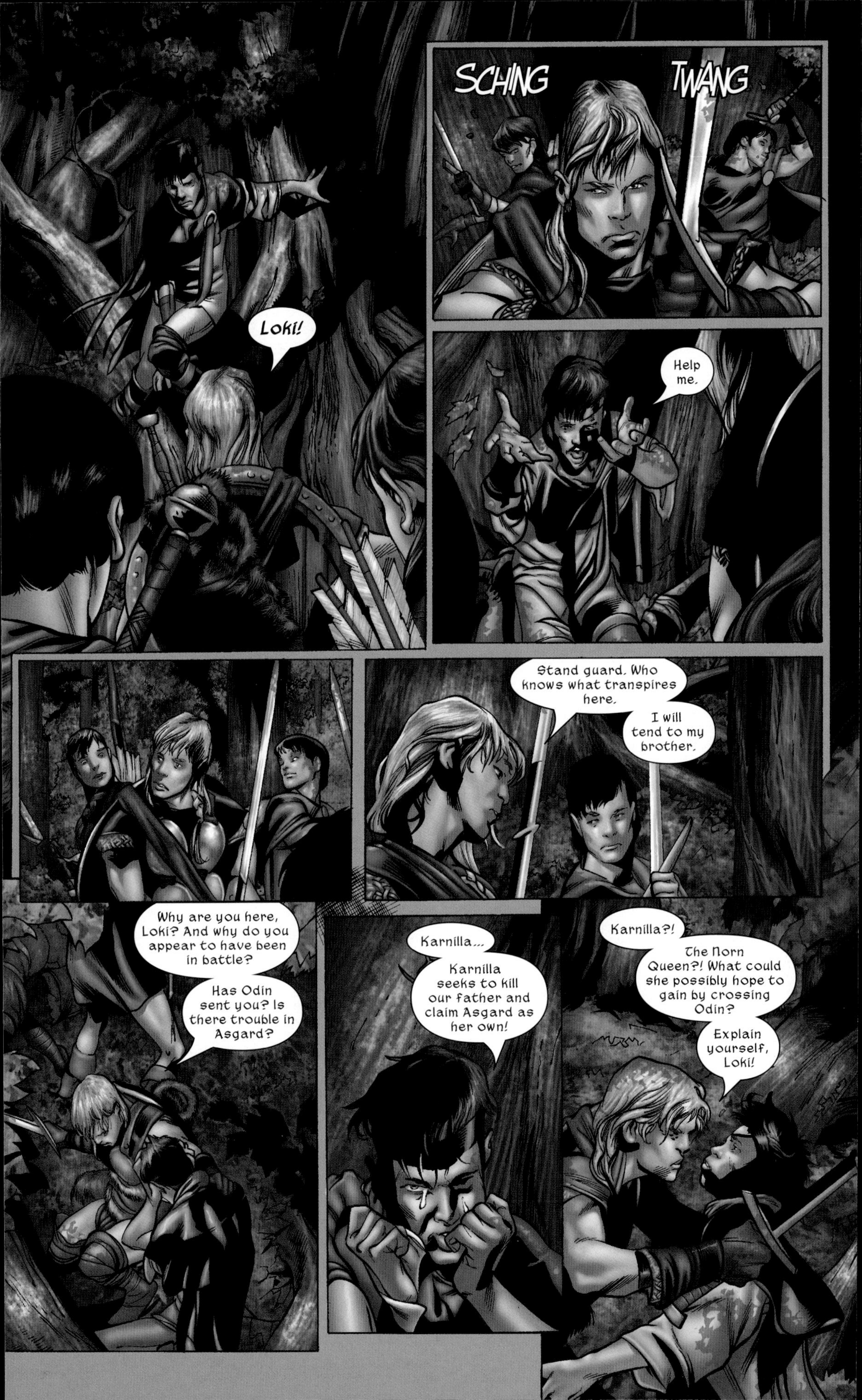
Loki!
SCHING
TWANG
Help me.
Stand guard. Who knows what transpires here.
I will tend to my brother.
Why are you here, Loki? And why do you appear to have been in battle?
Has Odin sent you? Is there trouble in Asgard?
Karnilla...
Karnilla seeks to kill our father and claim Asgard as her own!
Karnilla?!
The Norn Queen?! What could she possibly hope to gain by crossing Odin?
Explain yourself, Loki!

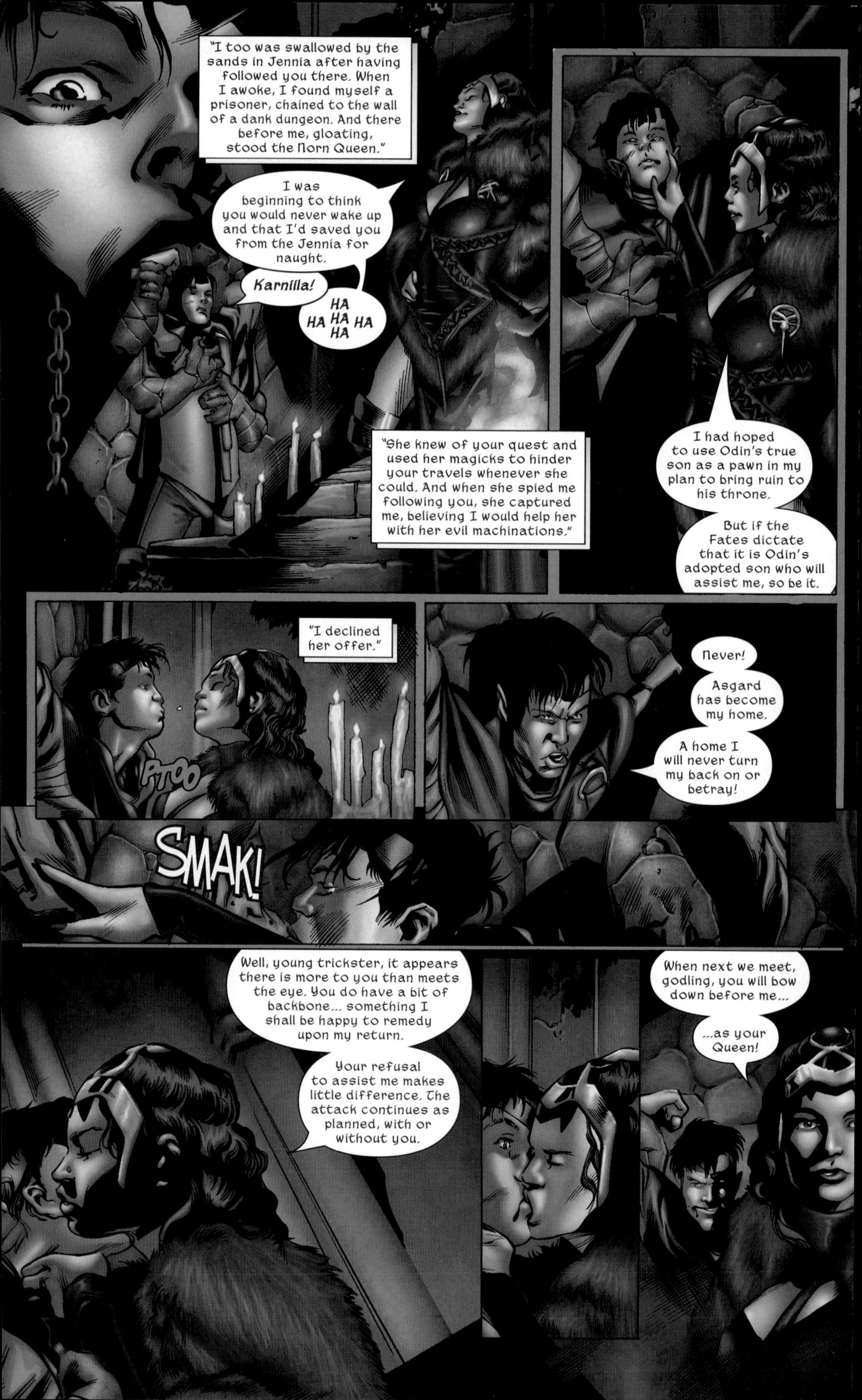

"I too was swallowed by the sands in Jennia after having followed you there. When I awoke, I found myself a prisoner, chained to the wall of a dank dungeon. And there before me, gloating, stood the Norn Queen."
I was beginning to think you would never wake up and that I'd saved you from the Jennia for naught.
Karnilla!
HA HA HA HA HA
"She knew of your quest and used her magicks to hinder your travels whenever she could. And when she spied me following you, she captured me, believing I would help her with her evil machinations."
I had hoped to use Odin's true son as a pawn in my plan to bring ruin to his throne.
But if the Fates dictate that it is Odin's adopted son who will assist me, so be it.
"I declined her offer."
PTOO
Never!
Asgard has become my home.
A home I will never turn my back on or betray!
SMAK!
Well, young trickster, it appears there is more to you than meets the eye. You do have a bit of backbone... something I shall be happy to remedy upon my return.
Your refusal to assist me makes little difference. The attack continues as planned, with or without you.
When next we meet, godling, you will bow down before me...
...as your Queen!

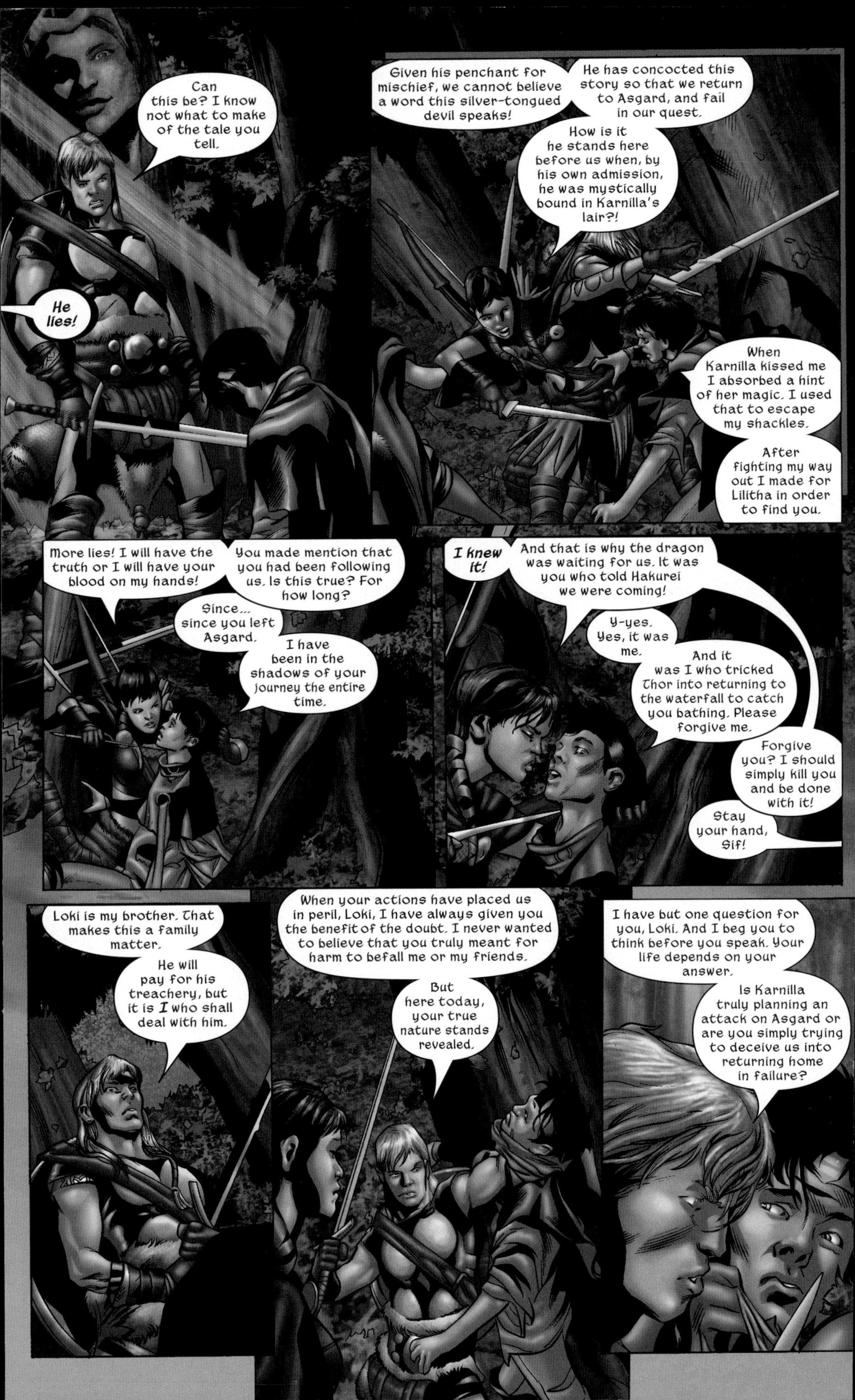
Can this be? I know not what to make of the tale you tell.
He lies!
Given his penchant for mischief, we cannot believe a word this silver-tongued devil speaks!
He has concocted this story so that we return to Asgard, and fail in our quest.
How is it he stands here before us when, by his own admission, he was mystically bound in Karnilla's lair?!
When Karnilla kissed me I absorbed a hint of her magic. I used that to escape my shackles.
After fighting my way out I made for Lilitha in order to find you.
More lies! I will have the truth or I will have your blood on my hands!
You made mention that you had been following us. Is this true? For how long?
Since... since you left Asgard.
I have been in the shadows of your journey the entire time.
I knew it!
And that is why the dragon was waiting for us. It was you who told Hakurei we were coming!
Y-yes. Yes, it was me.
And it was I who tricked Thor into returning to the waterfall to catch you bathing. Please forgive me.
Forgive you? I should simply kill you and be done with it!
Stay your hand, Sif!
Loki is my brother. That makes this a family matter.
He will pay for his treachery, but it is I who shall deal with him.
When your actions have placed us in peril, Loki, I have always given you the benefit of the doubt. I never wanted to believe that you truly meant for harm to befall me or my friends.
But here today, your true nature stands revealed.
I have but one question for you, Loki. And I beg you to think before you speak. Your life depends on your answer.
Is Karnilla truly planning an attack on Asgard or are you simply trying to deceive us into returning home in failure?

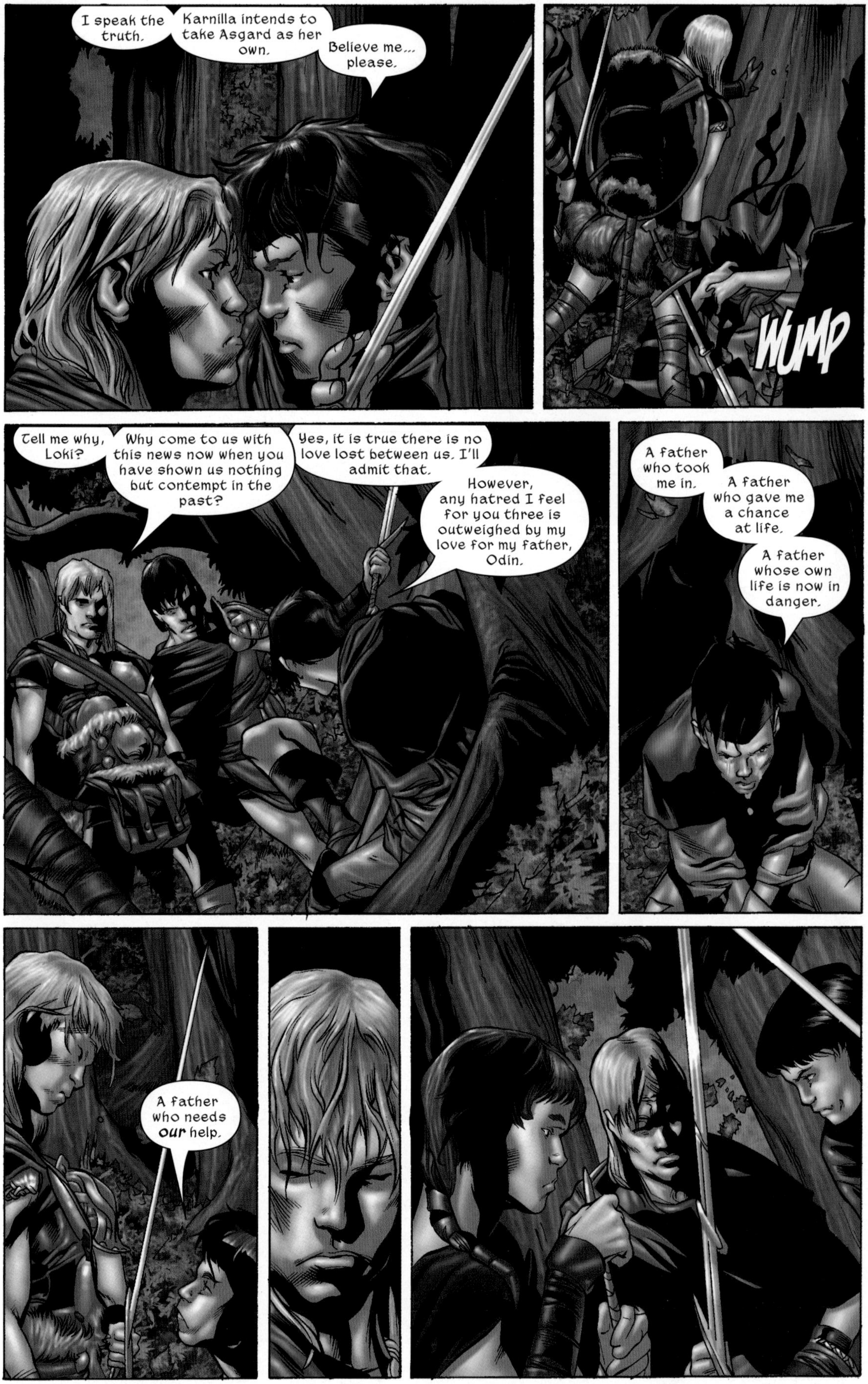

I speak the truth.
Karnilla intends to take Asgard as her own.
Believe me... please.
WUMP
Tell me why, Loki?
Why come to us with this news now when you have shown us nothing but contempt in the past?
Yes, it is true there is no love lost between us. I'll admit that.
However, any hatred I feel for you three is outweighed by my love for my father, Odin.
A father who took me in.
A father who gave me a chance at life.
A father whose own life is now in danger.
A father who needs **our** help.

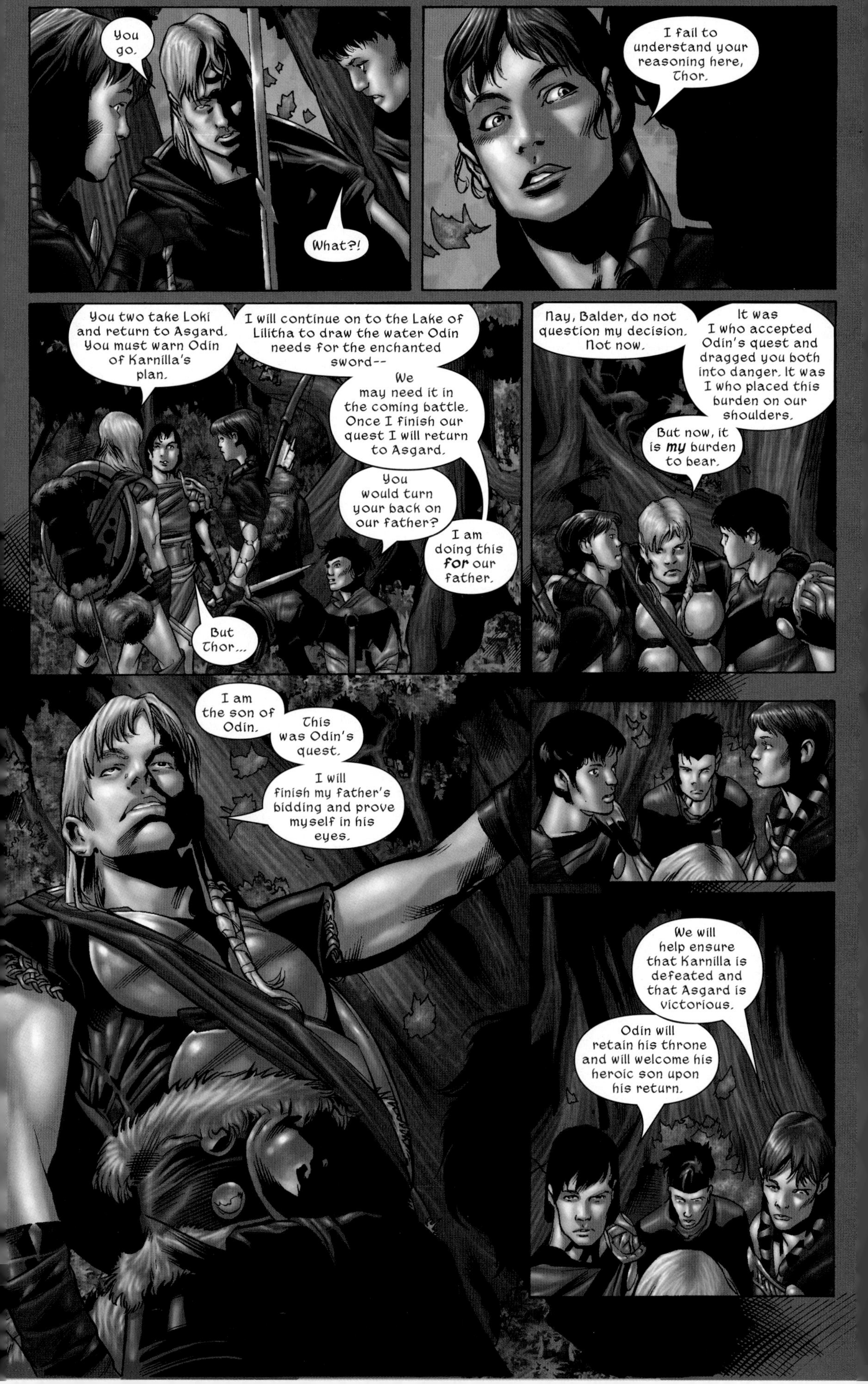
You go.
What?!
I fail to understand your reasoning here, Thor.
You two take Loki and return to Asgard. You must warn Odin of Karnilla's plan.
I will continue on to the Lake of Lilitha to draw the water Odin needs for the enchanted sword--
We may need it in the coming battle. Once I finish our quest I will return to Asgard.
But Thor...
You would turn your back on our father?
I am doing this **for** our father.
Nay, Balder, do not question my decision. Not now.
It was I who accepted Odin's quest and dragged you both into danger. It was I who placed this burden on our shoulders.
But now, it is ***my*** burden to bear.
I am the son of Odin.
This was Odin's quest.
I will finish my father's bidding and prove myself in his eyes.
We will help ensure that Karnilla is defeated and that Asgard is victorious.
Odin will retain his throne and will welcome his heroic son upon his return.

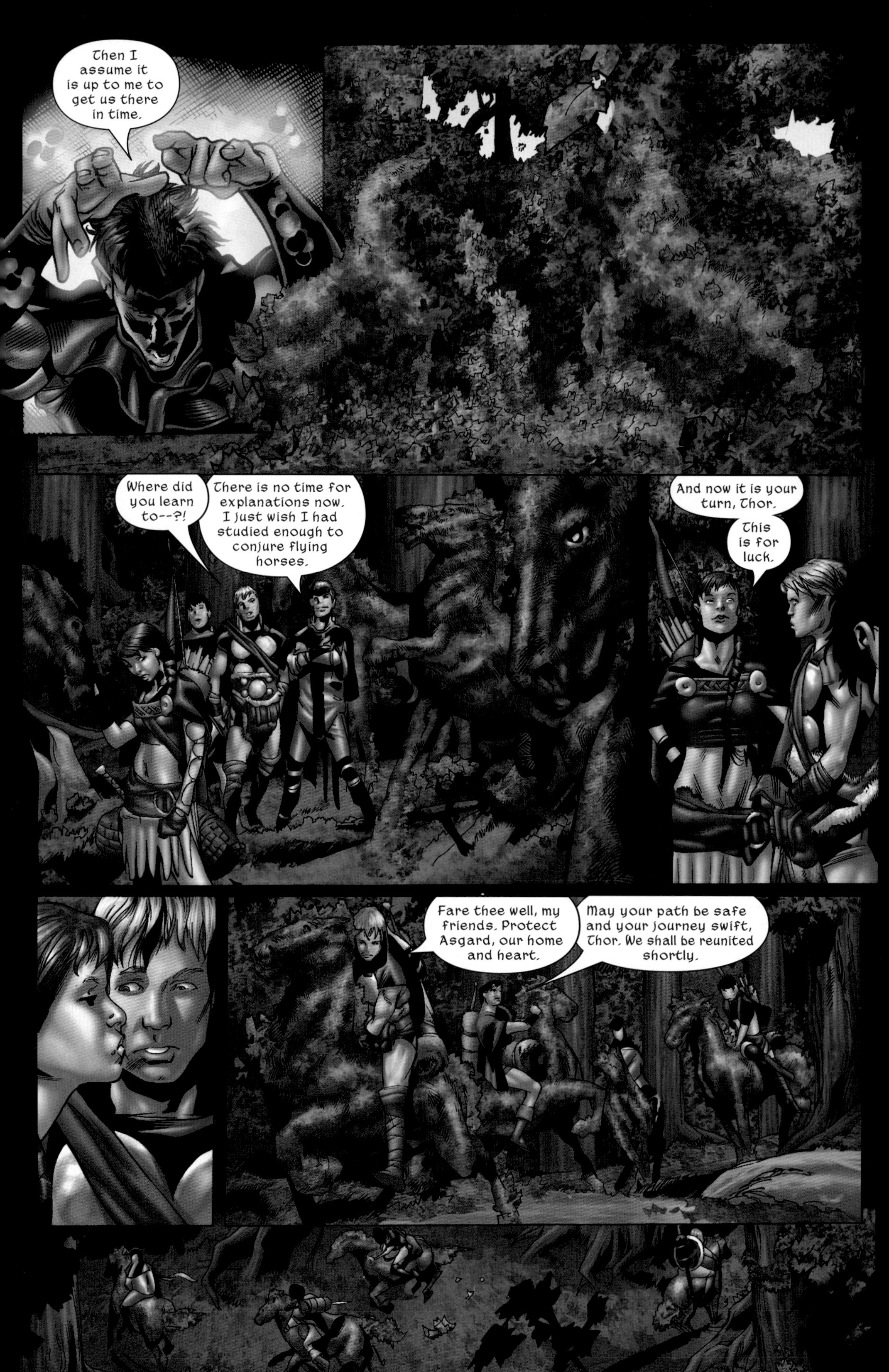
Then I assume it is up to me to get us there in time.
Where did you learn to--?!
There is no time for explanations now. I just wish I had studied enough to conjure flying horses.
And now it is your turn, Thor.
This is for luck.
Fare thee well, my friends. Protect Asgard, our home and heart.
May your path be safe and your journey swift, Thor. We shall be reunited shortly.

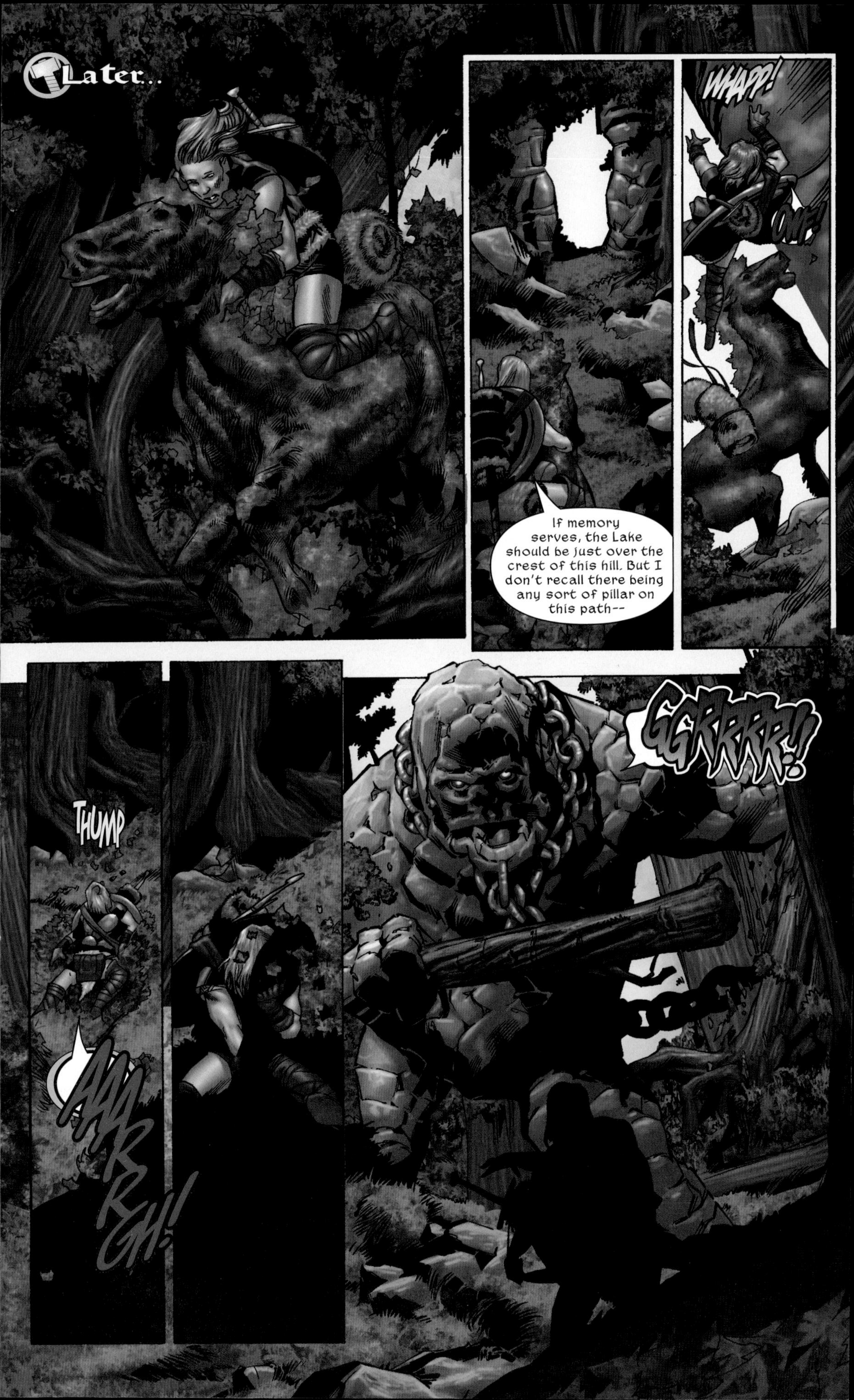
Later...
If memory serves, the Lake should be just over the crest of this hill. But I don't recall there being any sort of pillar on this path--
WHAPP!
OOF!
THUMP
AAARRGH!
GGRRRR!!

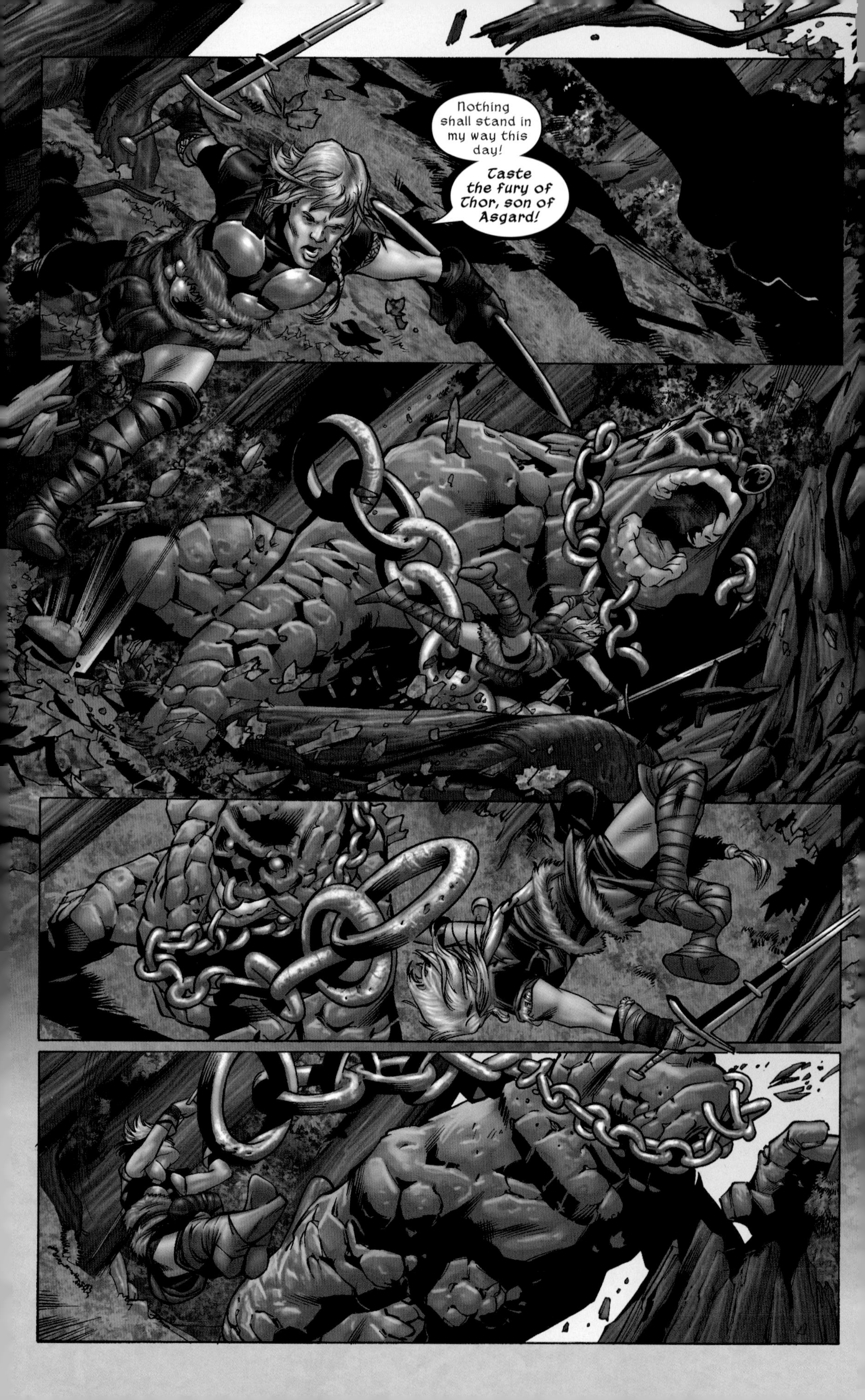
Nothing shall stand in my way this day!
Taste the fury of Thor, son of Asgard!

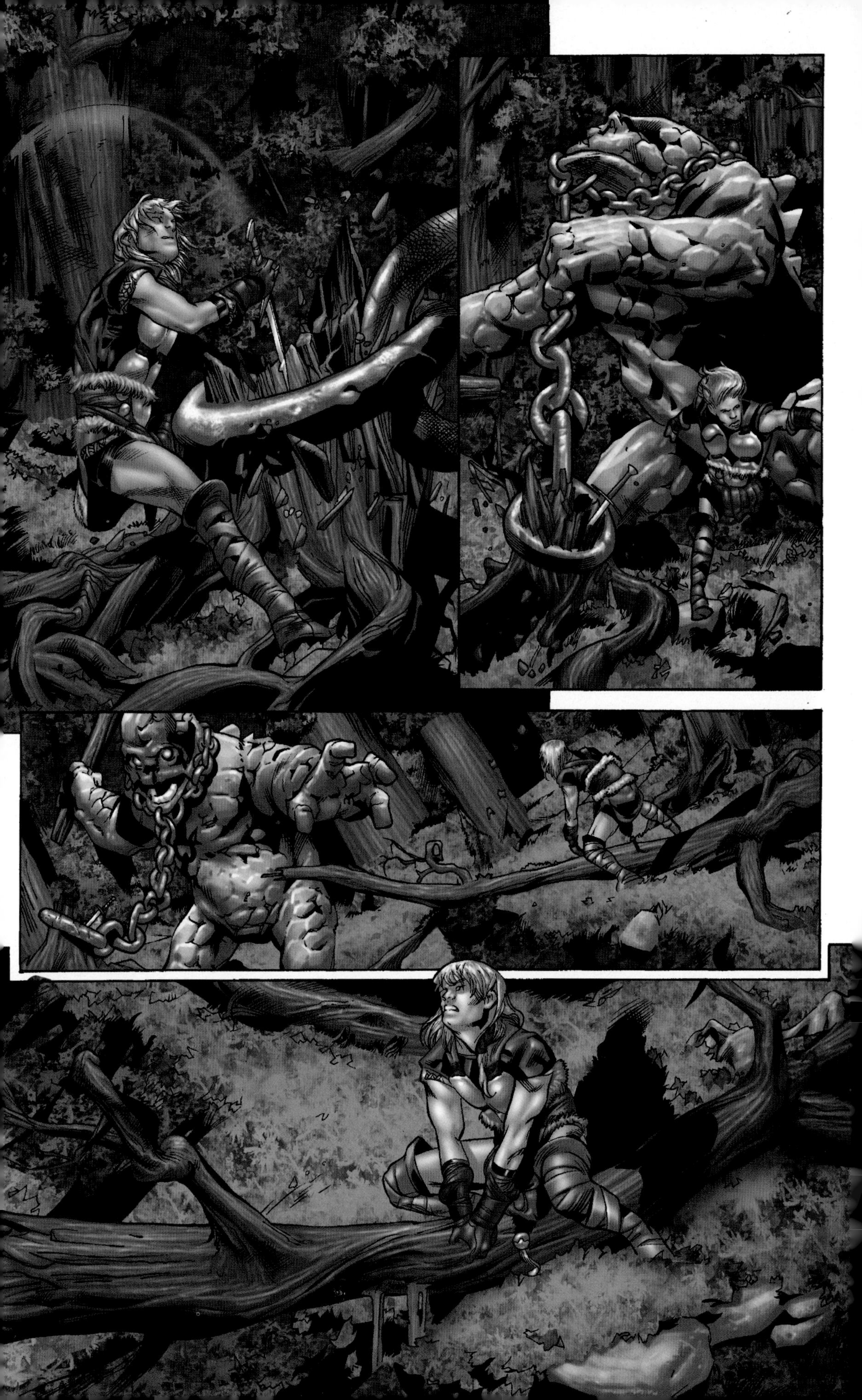

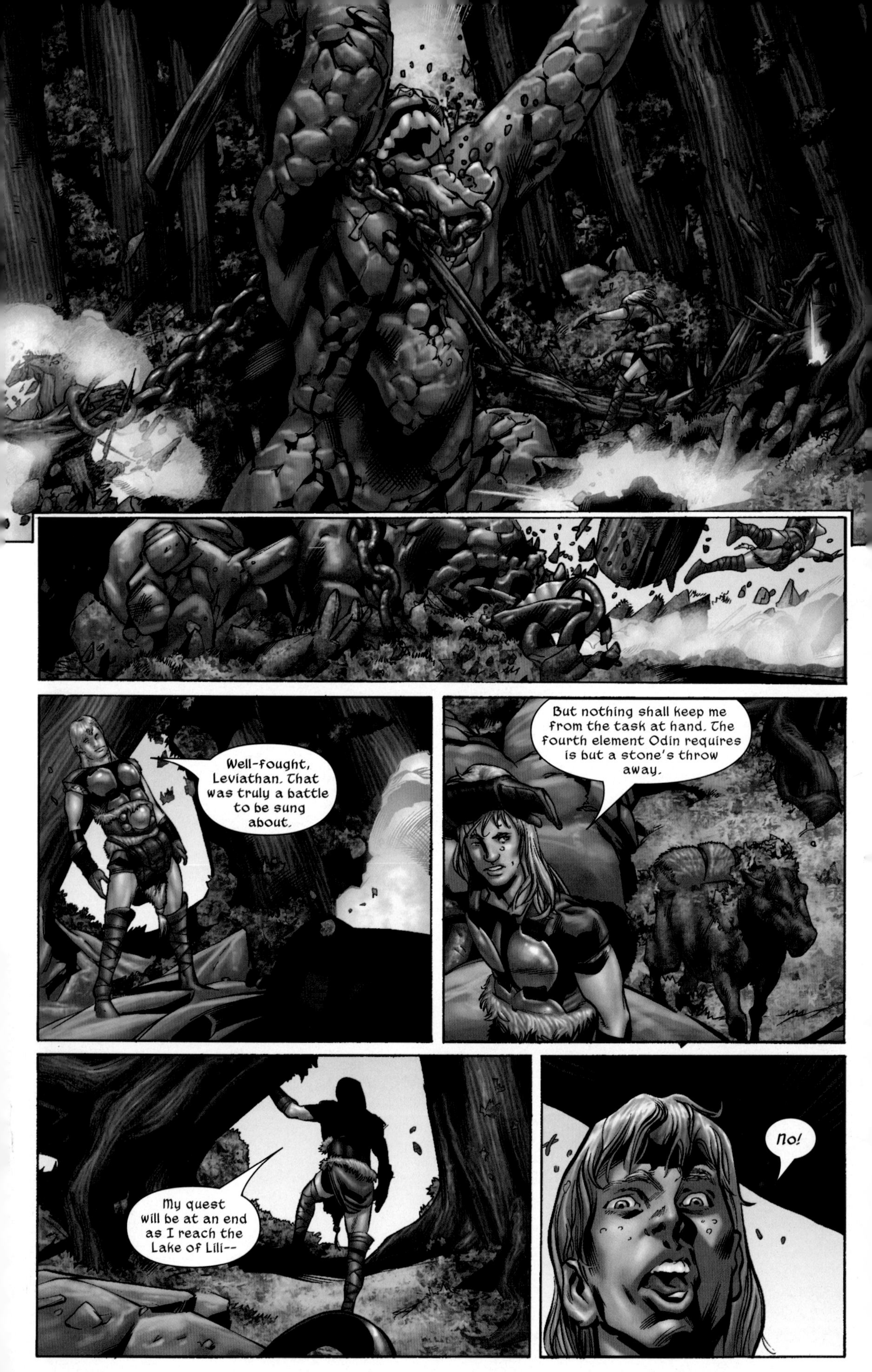

Well-fought, Leviathan. That was truly a battle to be sung about.
But nothing shall keep me from the task at hand. The fourth element Odin requires is but a stone's throw away.
My quest will be at an end as I reach the Lake of Lili--
No!

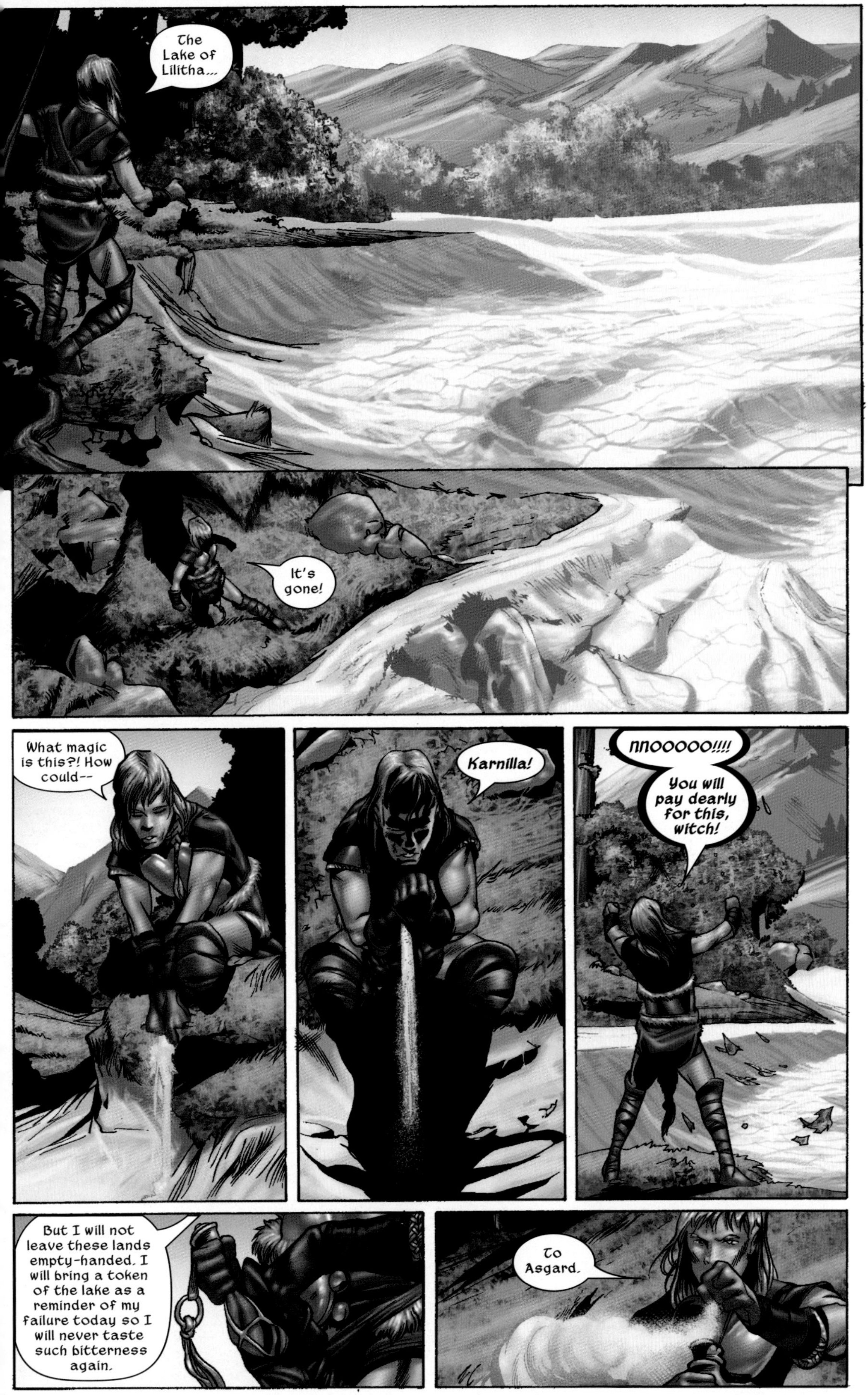
The Lake of Lilitha...
It's gone!
What magic is this?! How could--
Karnilla!
NNOOOOO!!!!
You will pay dearly for this, witch!
But I will not leave these lands empty-handed. I will bring a token of the lake as a reminder of my failure today so I will never taste such bitterness again.
To Asgard.

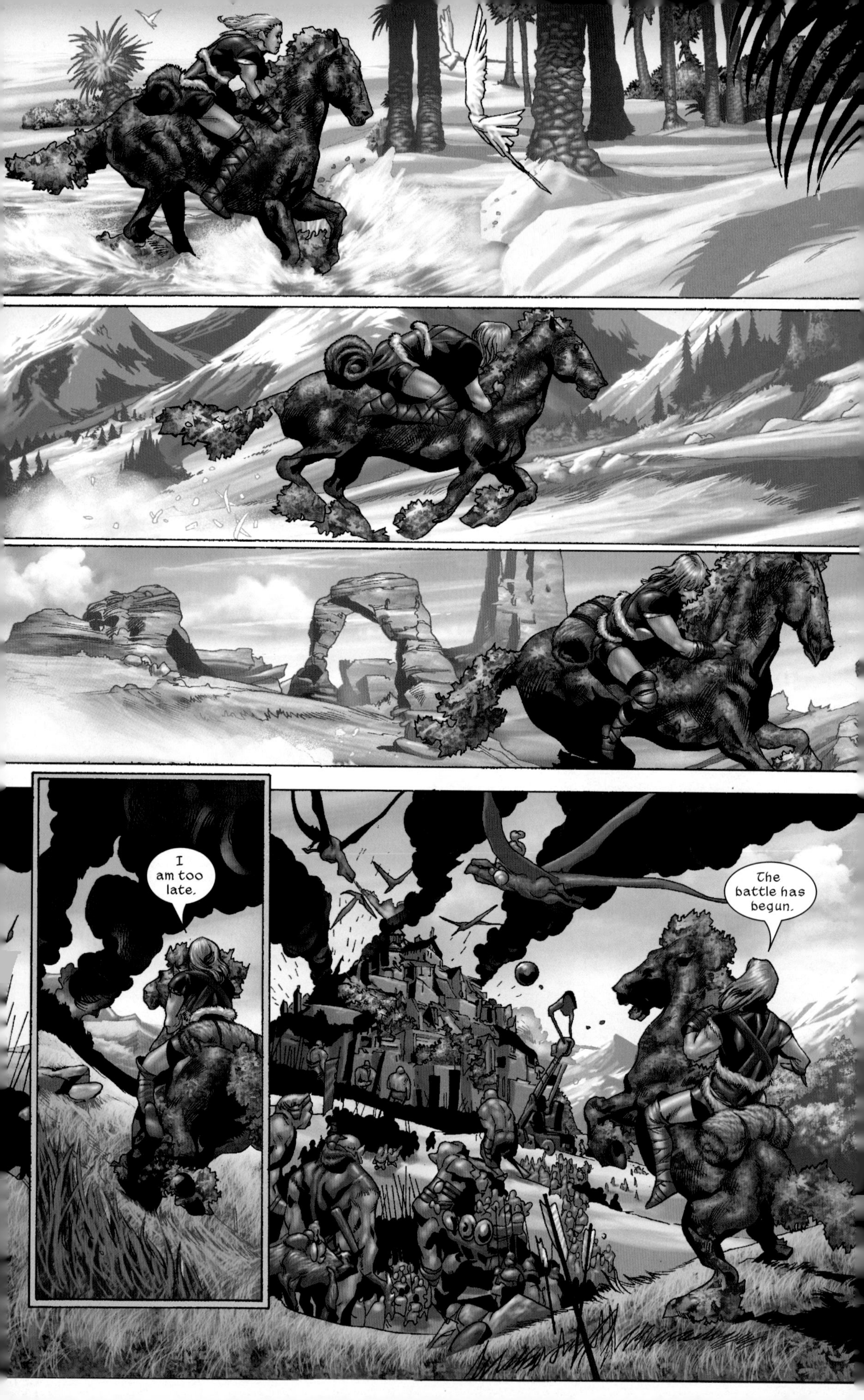
I am too late.
The battle has begun.

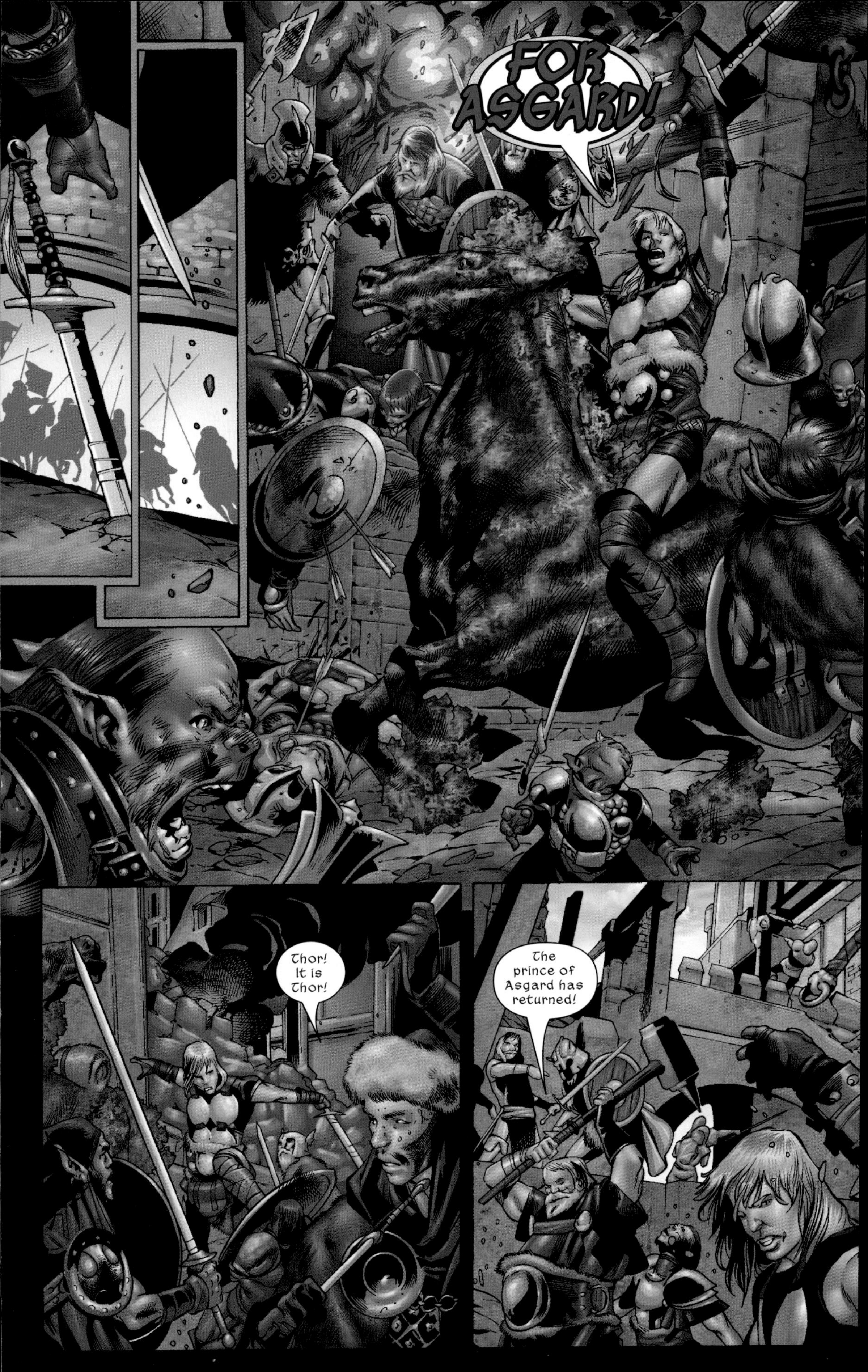
FOR ASGARD!
Thor! It is Thor!
The prince of Asgard has returned!

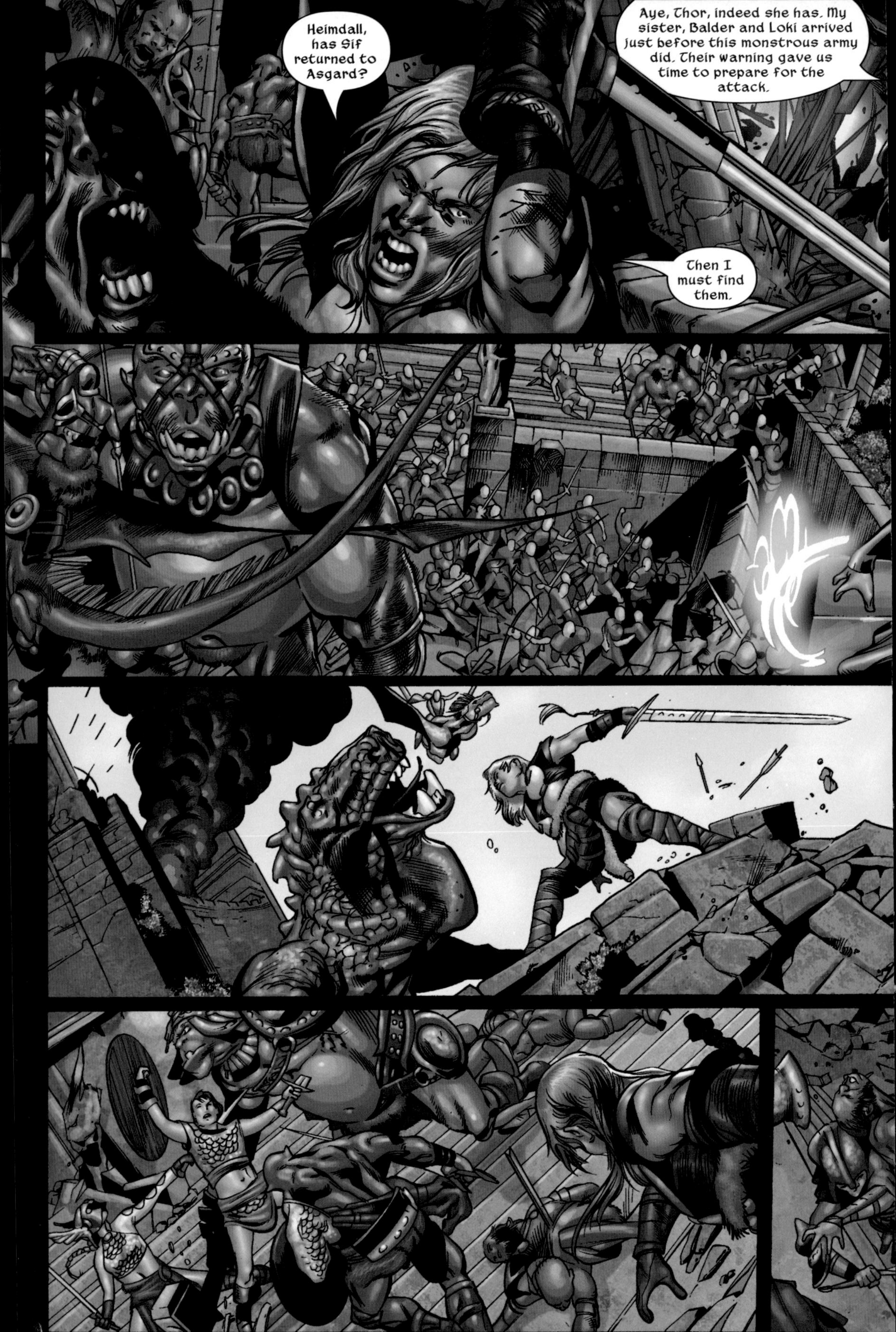
Heimdall, has Sif returned to Asgard?
Aye, Thor, indeed she has. My sister, Balder and Loki arrived just before this monstrous army did. Their warning gave us time to prepare for the attack.
Then I must find them.

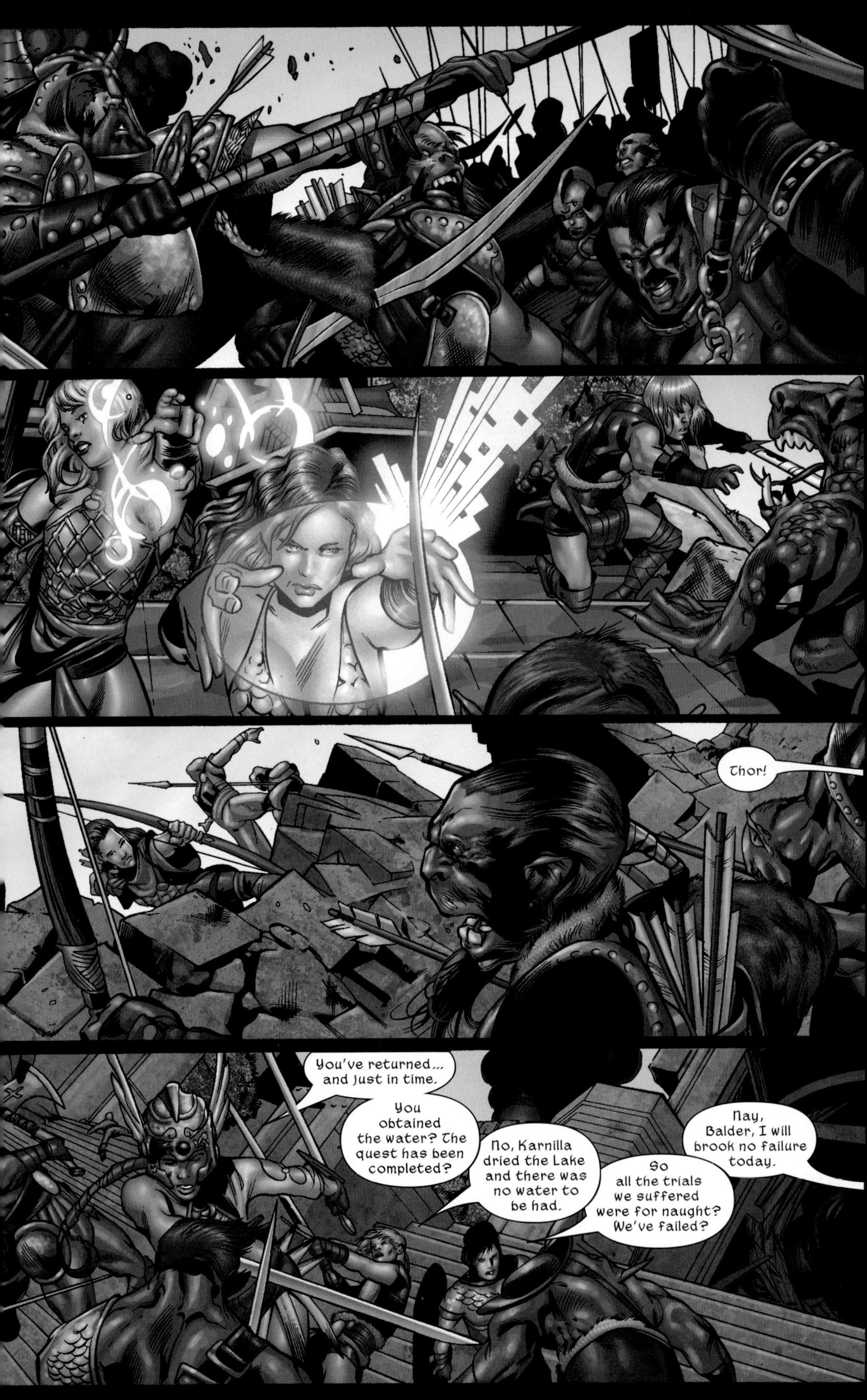
Thor!
You've returned... and just in time.
You obtained the water? The quest has been completed?
No, Karnilla dried the Lake and there was no water to be had.
So all the trials we suffered were for naught? We've failed?
Nay, Balder, I will brook no failure today.

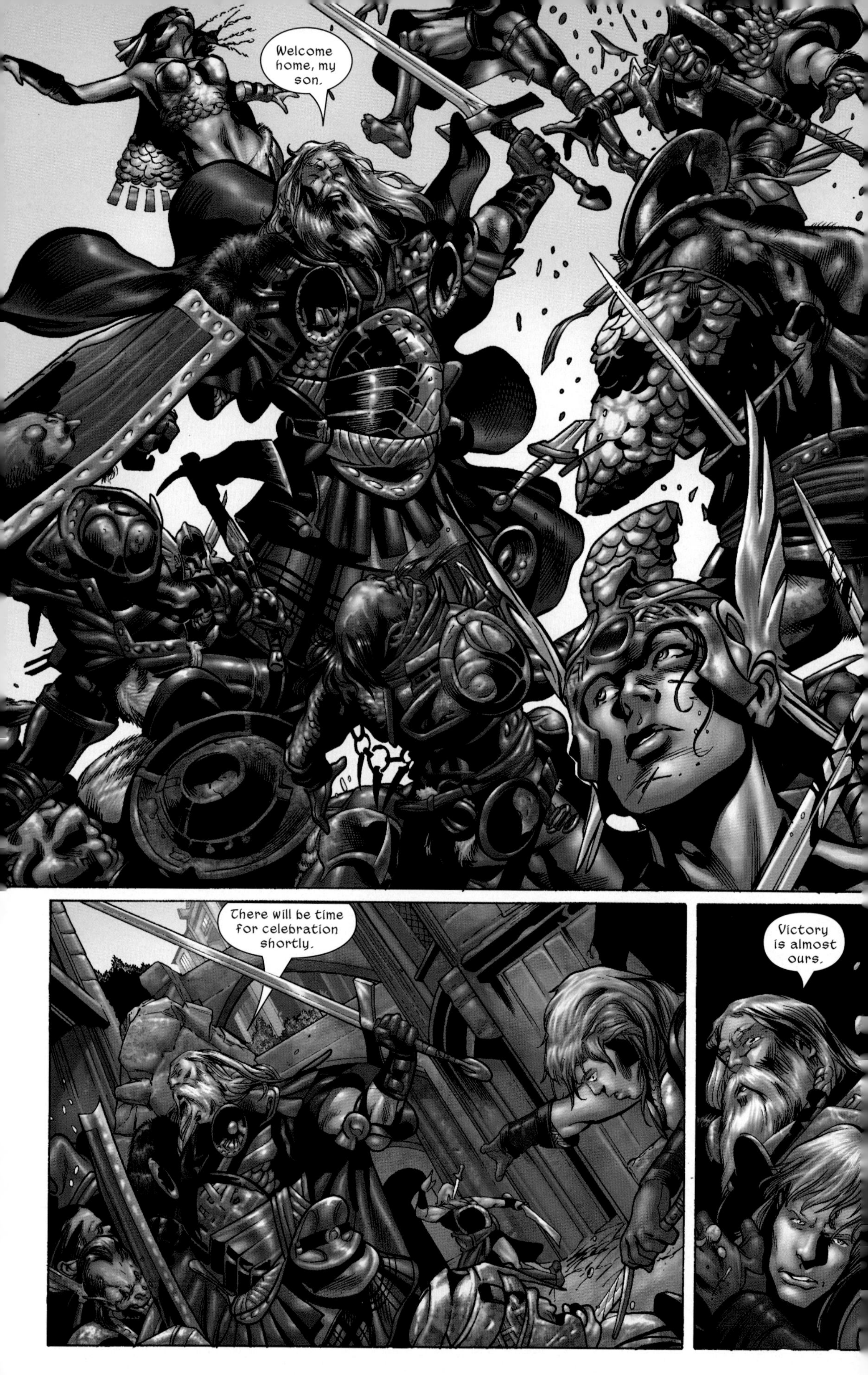
Welcome home, my son.
There will be time for celebration shortly.
Victory is almost ours.

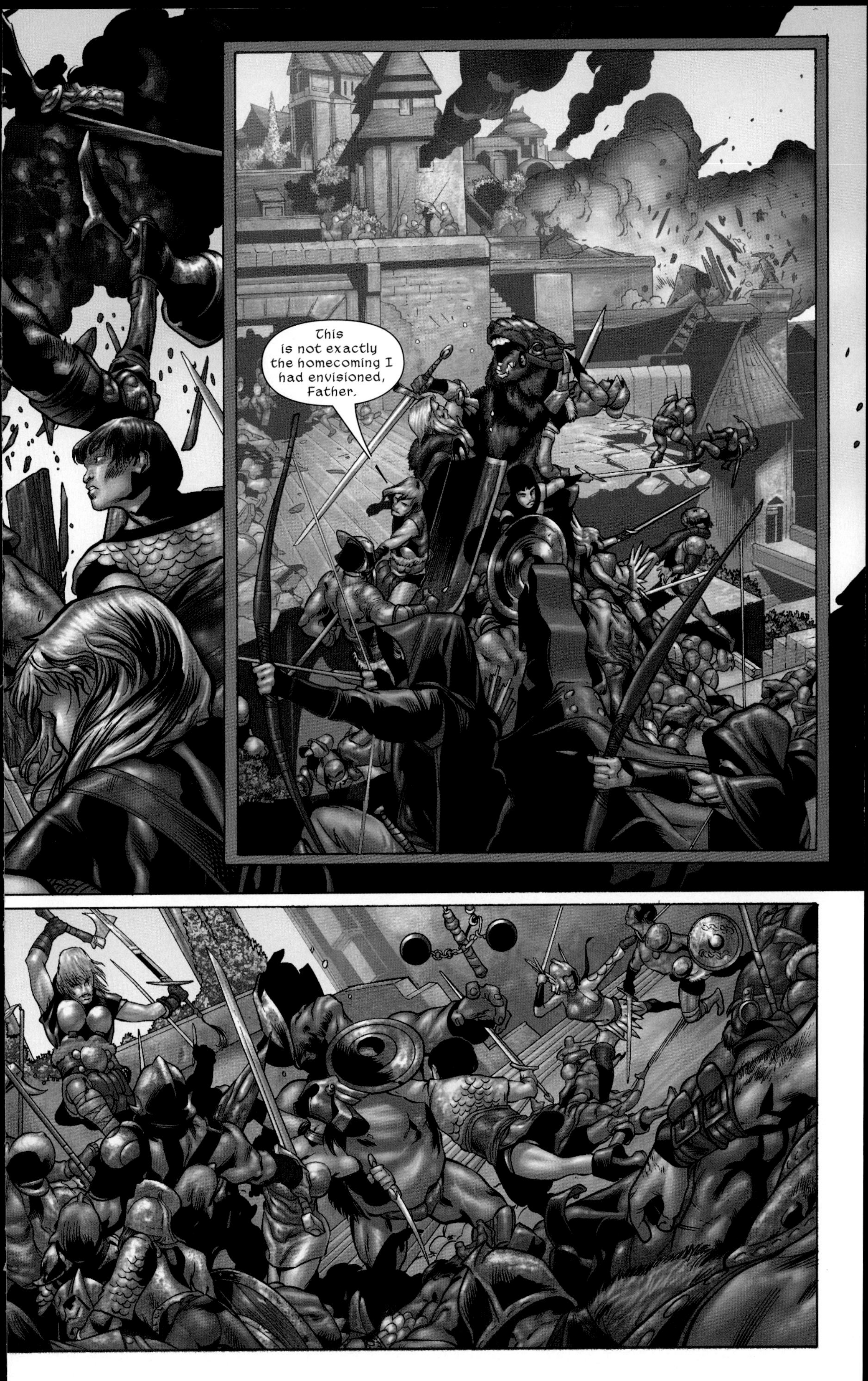
This is not exactly the homecoming I had envisioned, Father.

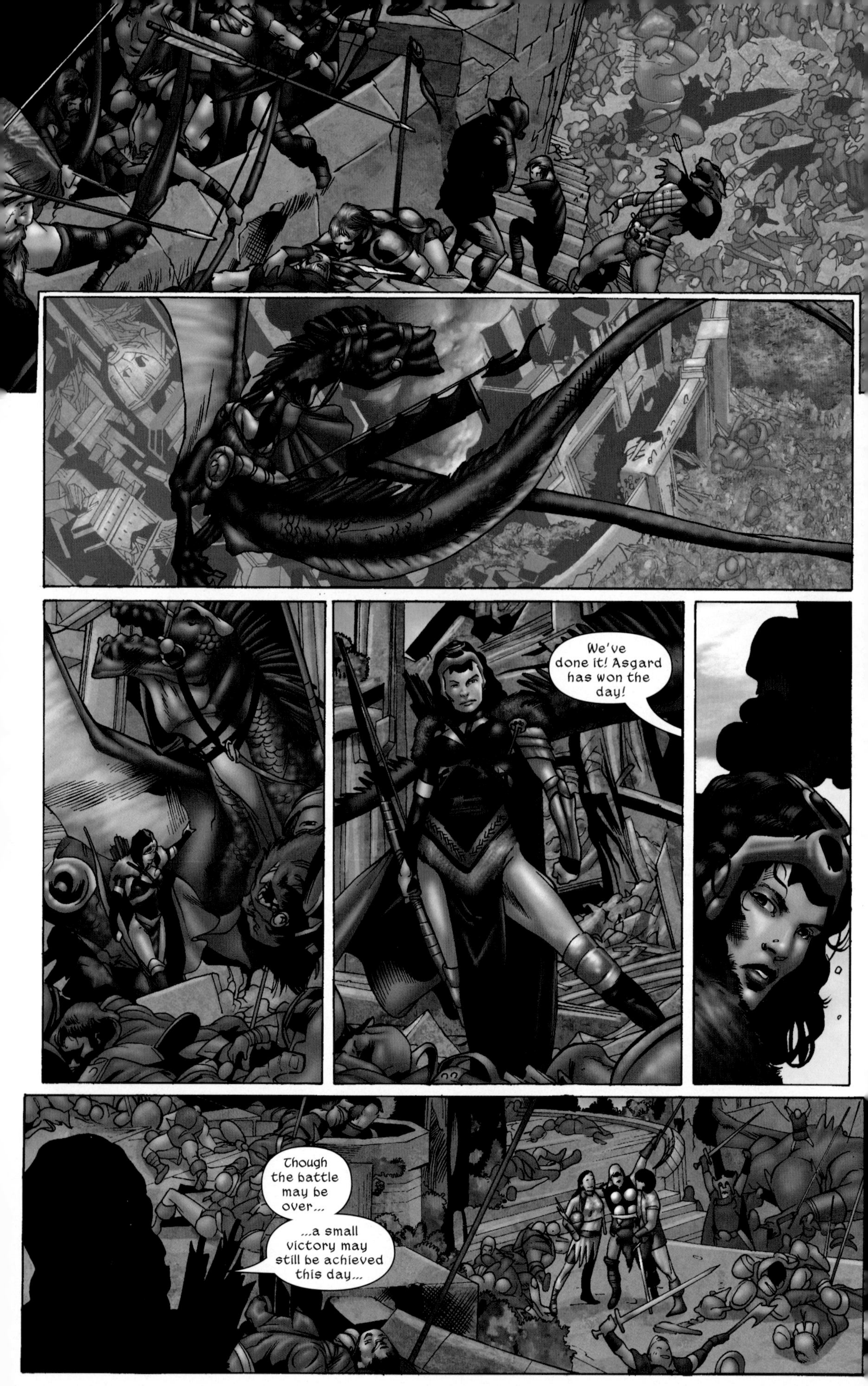
We've done it! Asgard has won the day!
Though the battle may be over...
...a small victory may still be achieved this day...

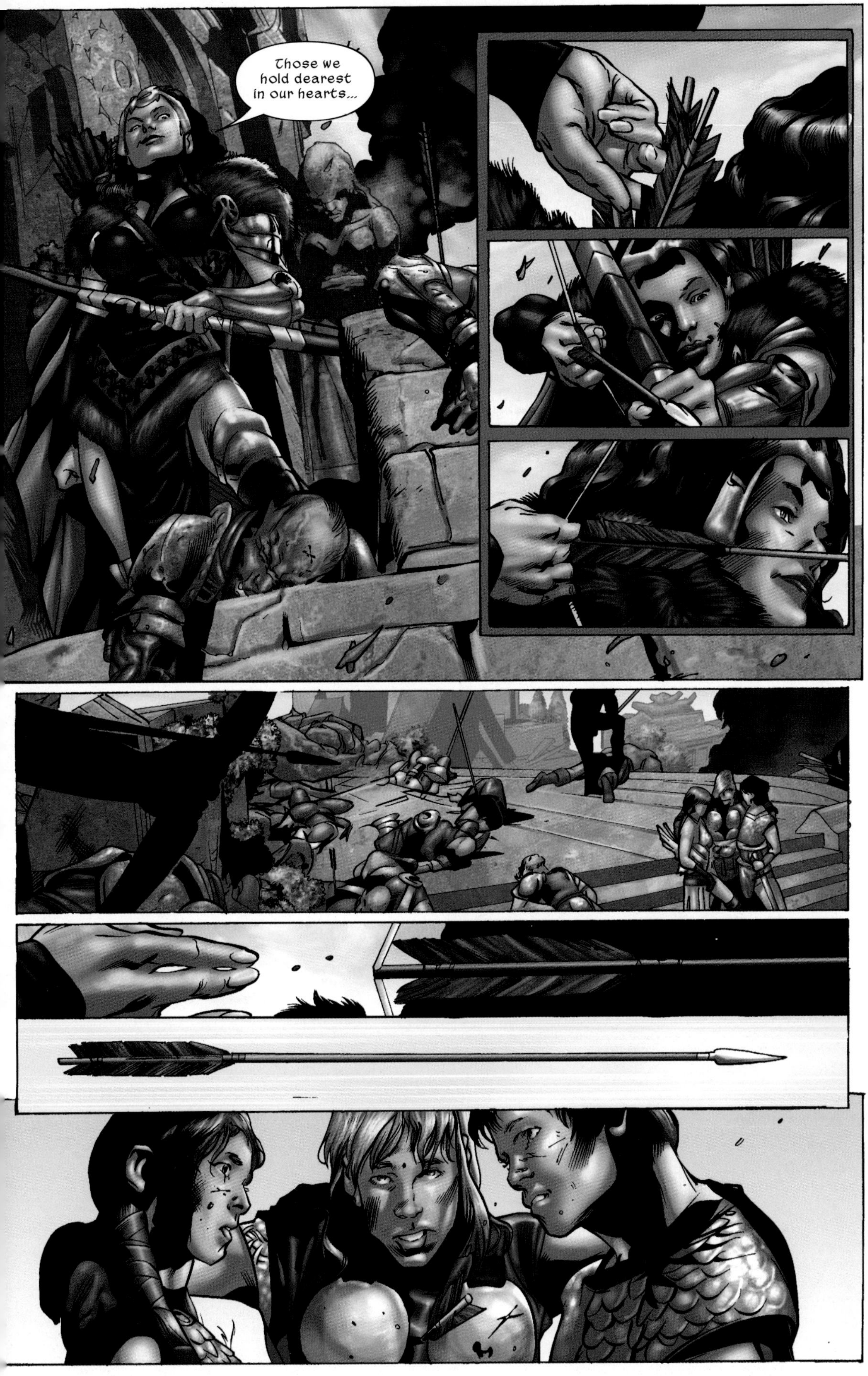
Those we hold dearest in our hearts...

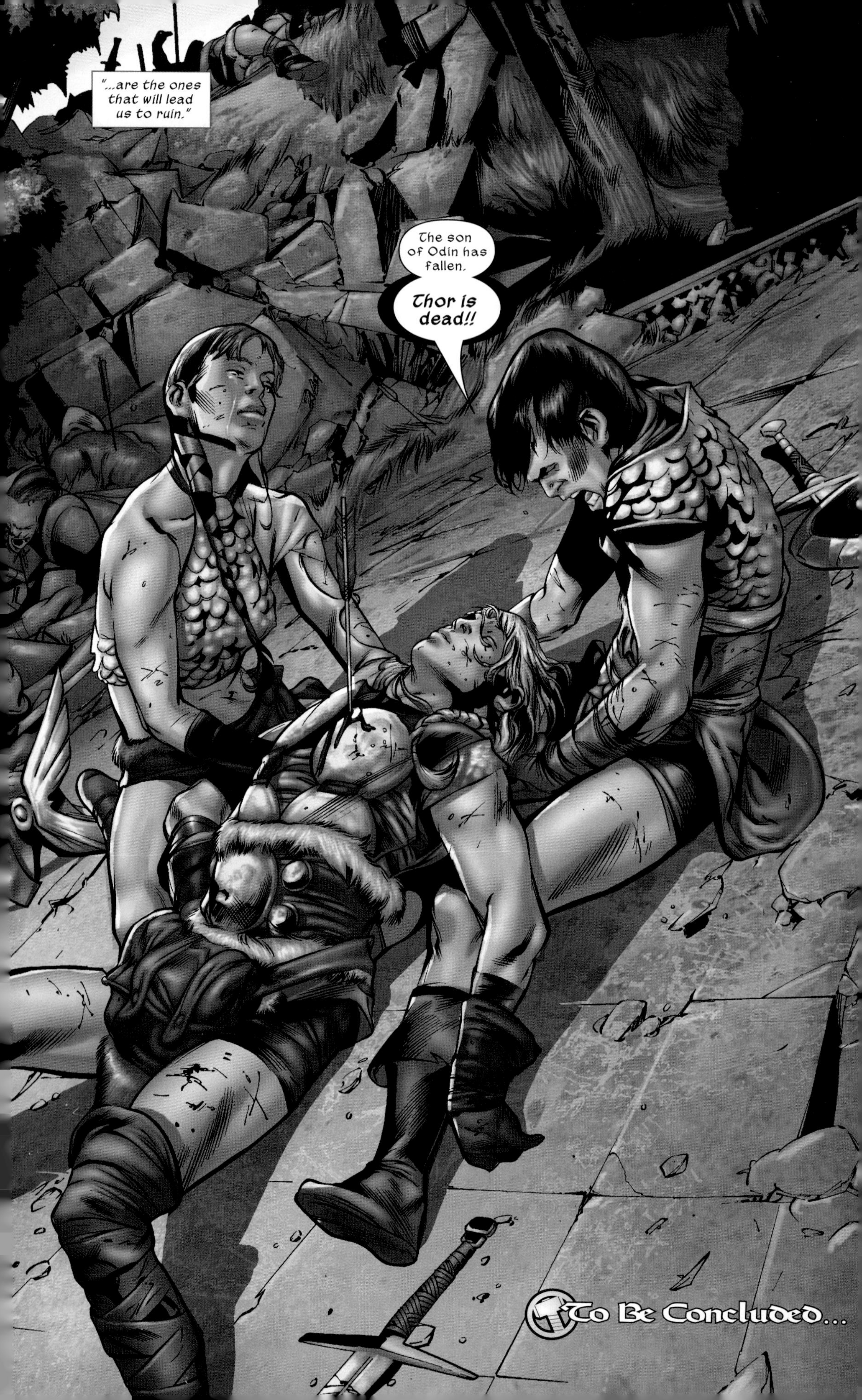

"...are the ones that will lead us to ruin."
The son of Odin has fallen.
Thor is dead!!
To Be Concluded...